MY FULL MOON IS SQUARE

BY ELINOR J. PINCZES
ILLUSTRATED BY RANDALL ENOS

Houghton Mifflin Company Boston 2002

With love to my sister, Ethie. Thanks —E.J.P.

For my little friend, Hannah Leigh MacDonald —R.E.

Text copyright © 2002 by Elinor Pinczes
Illustrations copyright © 2002 by Randall Enos

www.houghtonmifflinbooks.com

The text of this book is set in 14-point Clarendon.
The illustrations are linocuts with colored overlays.

Library of Congress Cataloging-in-Publication Data

Pinczes, Elinor J.
My full moon is square / Elinor Pinczes ; illustrated by Randall Enos.
p. cm.
Summary: When the full moon over Peekaboo Pond is covered by a
cloudy haze, a bullfrog needs the fireflies' help so that he can continue
reading to them.
ISBN 0-618-15489-2 (hardcover)
[1. Bullfrog—Fiction. 2. Frogs—Fiction. 3. Books and reading—Fiction.
4. Fireflies—Fiction. 5. Stories in rhyme.] I. Enos, Randall, ill. II. Title.
PZ8.3.P558676 2002   [E]—dc21   2002000221

Manufactured in China
SCP 10 9 8 7 6 5 4 3 2 1

At Peekaboo Pond, there are many great features,
like cottonwoods, cattails, and curious creatures:
a bullfrog who'd finished a Learn-to-Read course
and a firefly swarm with its own power source.

Because of the noise on those fun days in June,
the frog read, out loud, by the light of the moon.

The flies would sneak down to their favorite limb
and hide in the leaves, while they listened to him.

Although they were fond of that frog's friendly face,
the swarm stayed a distance from him—just in case.

Their routine was changed in the weirdest of ways
when the full moon got lost in a thick, cloudy haze.

The bullfrog was squinting and starting to fret,
so the flies on the branches were getting upset.

"No moonlight tonight means no *Blue Kangaroo!*
Ho-hum, twiddle thumbs, now there's nothing to do."

"Oh, where is my moon?" the unhappy frog cried
as he closed his book, firmly, and placed it aside.

A brave group of flies, with their taillights aglow,
agreed they should help the poor bullfrog below.

The four thoughtful flies, in response to his need,
neatly hovered above, so the bullfrog could read.

Their total of four was the smallest of squares.
"How kind," said the frog to the two daring pairs.

"Ah, thanks for the gesture. I know you mean well,
but your two by two square is too small, I can tell."
He kicked up his flippers and wiggled his toes.
"Perhaps you'd be willing to add a few rows?"

Their next square in size showed a total of nine.
The frog stared awhile at that brilliant design.

The bottom, the middle, and top each had three.
To figure this square, number three was the key.

"Good job," said the frog, as he picked up his book.
"It might do the trick," he said. "Let's have a look."

"Too small, once again," he said, wrinkling his nose.
"Could you come a bit closer or add to your rows?"

The fireflies figured they'd rather add more,
and lined up above him in four rows of four.

Their square, based on four, added up to sixteen.
"That's the prettiest pattern this frog's ever seen."

"You really are bright," he said, tapping his chin.
"But not bright enough, and I'd like to begin!"

Another group swooped in a loop-de-loop dive
until twenty-five lights were lined up, five by five.

He studied the square that was there on display.
"Going down or across I count five either way."

"The bigger, the better, and much brighter, too!
Now, I'll tell you the tale of that blue kangaroo."

The flies in the spotlight were showing no fear,
so the rest of the swarm began gathering near.

Their ten rows of ten, which had one hundred lights,
could have lit up the pond on the darkest of nights.

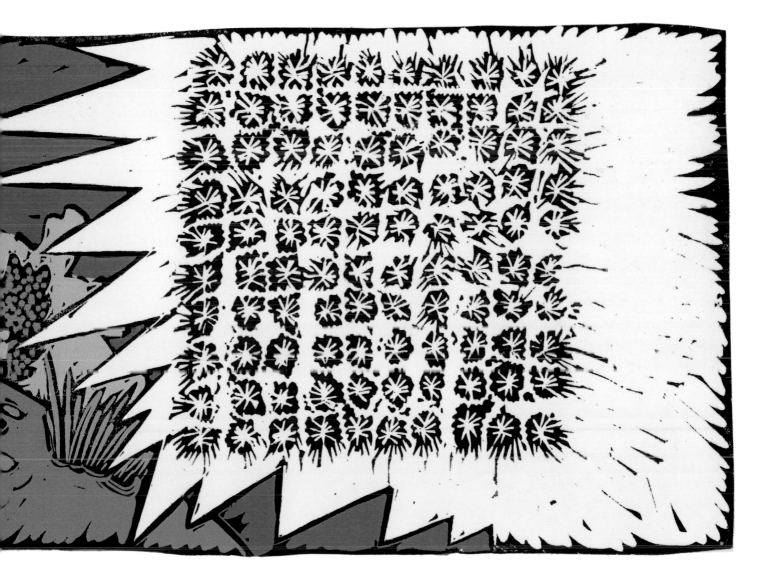

"Too big and too bright," said the frog. "I suppose...
you should move a bit higher or drop a few rows."

They chose to fly higher, which cut down the glare.
The happy frog chuckled, "My full moon is square!"

His square moon grew dimmer the longer he read.
"Well, enough for one sitting," the sleepy frog said.

"Tomorrow, at dusk, if we meet here once more—
whether cloudy or not, I can read chapter four!"

Their love of a good book had formed a strong bond.
That's why there's a square moon at Peekaboo Pond!